LEMONADE

LEMONADE

TOM ASHTON

I would like to dedicate this book to my Mum and Dad for their unwavering support throughout my writing career.

Tom Ashton is a short story writer and novelist from Barrow in Furness, Cumbria, UK, who holds a degree in Creative Writing from the University of Derby, has worked for both publishers and literary agencies, and has spoken at universities and literature festivals about his career. He has had three stories from his Grenton Village collection (set in South Cumbria) published since November 2018.

You can chat with Tom Ashton on Twitter: @thattomashton

Peter was short, round, and had a penchant for yellow, which made him suit his surname; Lemon, though he did not consider himself in any way a bitter man.

He even traded in lemons on occasion, being one of two greengrocers who co-owned Grenton Groceries, the best (and only) sellers of premium fruit and vegetables in Grenton Village, outside the villagers' own not-unproductive gardens, of course.

#

Peter was greeted by a strange view when he threw back his curtains. It was a view that contained bright sunshine, and did not include the furious raincloud that usually dominated the sky over South Cumbria.

Delighted by this environmental rarity, Peter flung himself into his morning ablutions and hurried outside, although, he still took extra special care to mind the yellow paintwork of his front door as he closed it. His door was one of his favourite features of a house he adored; a house he'd purchased for a reasonable price a little over five years ago from a lady called Gina, who'd been in a hurry to move in with her boyfriend on nearby Grally Island. Peter had already known Gina a little, from the checkouts down Guernsey Road, but he hadn't known her rather-new, rather-young, rather well-paid, boyfriend, who'd apparently worked out of sight, in the stockroom of the independent retailer, before becoming an engineer.

Their relationship had come to a violent conclusion, if the Grenton Gazette was to be believed, but it rarely was, and Peter didn't know the woman that well after all, so he didn't pay too much attention to the gossip.

No, he was more than content with the house she'd sold him, particularly as it was next door to Number 4, a striking residence known as 'The Green House', renowned for having the most beautiful front garden in Grenton. However, Gerald, the owner of Number 4, wasn't just a revered member of Green Lane for his gardening skills, oh no, he consistently provided something almost as valuable.

If the villagers of Grenton stood near Gerald's garden for any length of time, they could be assured that they would be colourfully dismissed by the old man.

A pretty garden and someone to moan about; what more could a pair of friends, on an afternoon stroll, ask for?

Peter thought the garden bloomed particularly bright that day, and dared to pause a little longer than usual to lean over the man's front gate and scratch the left ear of his Jack Russell, Bert; a sociable hound who spent much of his day watching the comings and goings of Green Lane through his favourite gap in the wood.

Peter enjoyed Bert's company for a full minute, before the dog shot off, responding to a gruff summons from somewhere beyond the wedged-open front door of Number 4.

Dr Darley, Grenton's veterinarian, had once assured the patrons down the Bay Horse, that Bert was happier than most people he'd met, and that they should not suspect Gerald of treating the dog with the same disdain with which he treated everyone else. Since then, it had been understood that the only thing Gerald loved more than his garden, was his dog.

Peter smiled once more over the ogre's prized roses then set off on his way, feeling he'd pushed his luck for long enough. He waved to Gustavo the Postman, who nodded in reply, whilst juggling a cup of coffee and several packages between his hands, as he hurried across the street.

Peter was about to suggest to Gustavo, who'd looked exhausted ever since the strikes had begun, that he should take some time off, but was denied the opportunity by the sudden appearance of Mrs Higgins from the corner, who began a passionate tirade about the fee Mr Sprout was charging for exterminating the church's rats.

"I know he's the best at what he does," she said, "But we're a church! It's daylight robbery, for Pete's sake."

"Hey, you leave me out of it." He winked and her face filled with delight, and off she went, back to her post on the corner, to recount their exchange to Mrs Smith and Dr Parker. Peter knew his quip would become her quip by its third re-telling but he wasn't bothered. It was a wonderful day.

He arrived at work an hour and ten minutes early, and was not surprised to find his business partner Aidan O'Sullivan already there, scrubbing the shop window within an inch of its life. He saw Peter coming in the sparkling glass and broke into a grin.

"Lemon!" He said.

"Ade!" Peter replied.

"Don't mind if I do!" They chortled in unison, thus completing their morning ritual.

Most of the time Ade arrived for work very early. Peter arrived a mere twenty minutes before they opened, during which time he would whizz the stock out from the back, whilst Ade counted out the till. That had been the way it had always been, and neither of them had ever suggested to the other that the arrangement was in any way unsuitable.

"Why are you here so early, Pe…" Ade began, before he was interrupted by a burst of drilling from somewhere behind the shop.

"What the heck's that?" Said Ade, "Is it coming from the yard?"

"I shall go and investigate." Said Peter, "You get these windows finished young G…G… Granville, or you might consider your apprenticeship here in jjj… jeopardy."

Ade chuckled and rolled his eyes. He was fifty-seven, whereas Peter was still a spritely fifty-three.

"Take them bags of old cabbages round to the bins with you, will you? They're getting stinky even for our stockroom."

Peter lifted the four squidgy black bin bags by the front door and grimaced as he caught a whiff of their contents. That was a lot of wasted green, and he wasn't talking about the cabbages. He made a mental note to become more involved in the procurement side of things in future, as he suspected Dempsey Pouge, a farmer Ade occasionally bought from, of playing on his fellow Irishman's good nature, as well as their shared heritage, to flog him shoddy wares and get away with it.

Peter puffed round the shop and found several men in orange hi-vis jackets and yellow hard-hats digging a big hole in the abandoned yard.

"Hello, Edgar." Said Peter, recognising a lanky labourer struggling with a wheel barrow full of chipped concrete. The boy's name was Edgar Wobble, son of the landlady of the Bay Horse, where he and Ade played chess some evenings. The boy had been working there as a glass collector when Peter had last seen him.

"New job, young man?"

"Alright Pete." Said Edgar, seizing the opportunity to dump down the wheelbarrow and prop himself up against it. "Yeah, just until I figure something out."

"I see." Said Peter, raising an eyebrow at him, "Out of interest, how come you're digging up the yard?"

Edgar frowned.

"I'm not insinuating this yard belongs to us, mind, I know it belongs to the council" Said Peter, flinging the black bin bags into the dustbin, "Just curious."

"Busted water pipe." Said Edgar, "Old Pouge the Rogue's been moaning that he's had nothing but mucky water down there for the last three weeks."

That explains the condition of those cabbages, thought Peter, and groaned as the bin bags rolled back out of the overflowing dustbin.

"Looks like our stockroom's going to stink for another week." Said Peter.

"Oi, Edgar Wobble," Shouted the foreman, "You better get back to work or I'll give your 'ed a wobble, lad!"

Edgar seized hold of his wheelbarrow again as the other men began laughing.

"Chuck them bin bags in the hole," he said, "we'll be back tomorrow to fill it in with tarmac anyhow."

Peter looked down into the hole where sandwich wrappers and drinks cans had already begun to accumulate.

"Is that allowed?"

"Who cares?" Said Edgar, staggering with the wheelbarrow as his colleagues continued to laugh.

Peter was not reassured by the teen's attitude but, at the same time, holding on to the rotten cabbages for another week really would not do.

He placed the bin bags beside the overflowing bin for the time being, deciding to put the matter on hold, at least until all the builders had gone home.

He strolled back round to the shop entrance, where he expected to find Ade inside, humming a little tune as he rummaged through the contents of the safe, but instead he found him sitting on the kerb, long limbs all bent out of shape like a crumpled daddy long-legs. The shop behind him remained closed.

"Ade, what an earth is the matter?" Peter said.

Ade took a few moments to reply, staring with sunken eyes at his mobile phone, sighing a hurricane all the while.

"It's Norris." He said, "He's out of prison. He's coming to see me."

Peter, like everyone else in Grenton, knew all about Ade's younger brother, Norris. Back in the day, he'd been the man to get you things. Be it the fertilizer from North Korea you needed by next week or the seventy grams of cocaine you needed by lunchtime, he was your man. It was a combination of these enterprises that had eventually resulted in his incarceration eight years ago, that and stabbing poor PC Summers in the leg with a trowel at the Garden Centre. Peter had become friendly with Ade two years later and they'd gone into business six months after that.

Ade was not himself all morning, falling over his words, giving incorrect change, and almost chopping his finger off with the dicing knife at one point. Peter was just about to suggest he go and have a lie down, when the shop bell tinkled and Norris appeared, rushing into Ade's midst to shout "Ello Bruvvvaa!" and pull him into an embrace.

Peter digested the skinhead. He was even thinner than Ade, somewhere around forty, with twiggy arms covered in blotchy blue tattoos.

"How's the family business?" He said.

Family business? Thought Peter, reducing the size of the apple he was holding through the violence with which he had begun to polish it. What does he mean by that?

The man released Ade and swung round, as if sensing Peter's disdain.

"And you must be the guy who took my job?" He said, the gaunt smile vanishing in an instant.

Ade stepped round between them. "Norris… it's not your job… this is Peter Lemon."

"Peter Lemon." Norris repeated, pushing Ade aside, seizing Peter's palm, and pumping his arm. It hurt and Peter could feel his fingers cracking.

"What do you do when life gives you lemons, eh?"

Peter opened his mouth and then closed it again. Ade grew paler.

"Norris… don't…" Ade said.

"I'm just messing." Norris laughed, releasing Peter's hand. "I just need somewhere to hole up for a few days until I can get back on my feet. You can do that for your little brother can't you, Aidan?"

He did it in that kind of sing-song voice a mother might use to manipulate her child into sharing a coveted toy with a sibling, and Peter wondered if it was an imitation of Mother O'Sullivan herself.

Ade shone wet eyes in Peter's direction. He reminded him of a stray whippet he'd once seen hanging around Grenton docks.

"Peter… just for a couple of days… he can have that tatty black sleeping bag we keep the brooms in…"

"Oh thanks." Said Norris, flapping his arms, "What you asking him for anyhow, it's your shop?"

"It's *our* shop." Peter said, feeling a similar defiance he'd not felt since senior school, when Albert Hagen had tried to take credit for his homework.

"As Peter says, Norris, it is *our* shop. Mine and his. OK?" Said Ade.
Norris' demeanour softened and he laughed. "Sure bro, I'm just messing."

He punched Peter hard on the arm, nearly knocking the little man over. "Mate, why are you so serious?"

"Peter, please, just a few days, then he'll be gone, I promise."

Peter looked at Ade, at the leering Norris, and then back at Ade. He wanted to tell Ade that under no circumstances was he willing to let this obnoxious criminal stay in the building that housed their livelihood, but that would look un-neighbourly. Plus, Norris might thump him one.

"Sure. Why not? Couple of days."

"Thank you." Ade said and pushed through the heavy plastic flaps that divided the shop from the stockroom.

"Maybe a week." Norris added, and went after his brother.

Adjacent to the stockroom was a greenhouse. Well, they referred to it as the greenhouse. It was an extension, made of congregated iron but with those translucent windows greenhouses have. Bit of an eyesore really, but they'd never got round to knocking it down. They'd never used it, and Peter was surprised Ade knew where the key was.

The O'Sullivans dragged the sofa from the office through the door that connected the greenhouse to the shop, and Norris was handed the old sleeping bag and told he could stay a few days provided he made himself useful, and he could start by cleaning out the old greenhouse. Norris promised to do his best and that he'd be out of Ade's hair soon (he said nothing about Peter) and then whisked his brother off to the Bay Horse for a 'Reunion drink'.

#

The following day Peter arrived at the shop to find Norris scrubbing the front window and Ade nowhere in sight.

"Where's Ade?"

Norris laughed and gestured behind him with his rag.

Meandering up the road towards Peter, was Ade, unshaven, hair all sticking up on one side, and face completely barren of his usual cheery temperament.

"Goodness me, Ade, are you ok?"

"He's fine. Just can't handle his ale. Never could."

"I only wanted one." Said Ade.

"We were celebrating!"

"Peter," Said Ade, "I'm so sorry… the shop…"

"Don't worry about that." Norris said, attacking a particularly resistant splodge of seagull poo, "I've already stocked the shelves and sorted the till out."

Both of the greengrocers looked at each other in panic and dashed inside.

Ade whacked opened the till and began counting, whilst Peter stalked the shelves.

After ten minutes or so, Norris strolled into the shop.

"It's all here." Ade said, looking up from the till.

"Shelves look alright." Said Peter.

"Of course." Said Norris, "Windows are done too. Now if you don't mind, I'll be off to the greenhouse to continue working in there."

Norris walked through the flaps and then stuck his head back inside.

"Lemon, Aidan has an excuse for being late, my coming home drinks and everything, but you should really try to make it to work earlier. It's not fair on your other colleagues."

"What do you mean 'colleagues'?" Peter said, fists balled up, "What business is it… ?" but he'd disappeared.

"I mean, it was good of him to come in and do all this…" Said Ade, "I'm impressed."

Peter turned towards him in horrified disbelief. "You're not serious?"

"What do you mean?"

"You know what he's like! He's just trying to worm his way in here!"

"I know he's my brother." Said Ade, "Are you saying ex-convicts shouldn't be given second chances?"

"No but… "

"He's impressed me today. He had the chance to clear out the shop and he didn't."

Ade walked towards the plastic flaps.

"And maybe he's right. It would be nice if you made the effort to get here a little earlier."

#

That evening when Peter arrived home, after a day of long silences, he plonked himself down on his yellow doorstep and stared at his shoes.

"Got yourself a rat in the shop, have ya?" Came a gruff Midlands voice from the other side of the fence, "They say Mr Sprout is the man to help you with that. Only I think your rat might be a little bigger than the ones he's used to dealing with."

Peter nearly fell off the step in surprise as he scrambled up to peer over the fence. Gerald was there turning the soil over with a spade, whilst Bert snored away by the rose bushes.

"Oh, good afternoon…" Peter said, struggling to find the words, "I hope the carrots we sold you this afternoon were to your satisfaction?"

Gerald stood up straight and looked him in the eye. He was old, very old, his face a knowing web of wrinkles, but he gave no aura of frailty. "They went very well in the stew Bert and I had for our tea." He said, "But I really came in for a look at that Norris. Heard the stories around. Some kind of big player back in the day apparently. I wasn't very impressed."

"He's Ade's brother..."

"He's also the purchaser of a lot of lighting equipment." Said Gerald, "Choi dropped it off in his van whilst you and your partner were on lunch. A lot of lighting and a lot of plants."

Peter was thinking hard. Choi. The man who'd stepped up to fill Norris' boots when he'd gone inside.

"What's he up to?"

"I wouldn't know." Gerald said and slapped the spade into Peter's hand. "You keep that. I've another. But this doesn't make us pals. And you leave Bert alone, you hear?"

He gave a short peep and Bert leapt up and trotted after his master. The door slammed behind them.

Peter looked at the spade, enamoured by their shared dislike of Norris, but confused by the man's actions. He should take the spade back up to the shop, he thought, if they couldn't find a use for it they could always sell it.

He knew he was really going back to the shop to check out the equipment Norris had ordered but the spade gave him an excuse. Wasn't he meant to be keeping a closer eye on procurement after the

Pouge Cabbage Incident anyway? Moreover, what right had Norris to order shop gear on their behalf, especially from that crook, Choi?

He was appalled to find the shop ablaze with light when he arrived, despite having turned every light off himself before he left not half an hour ago. His irritation intensified as heavy bass began thumping from within the depths of the shop. Think of the neighbours!

Peter unlocked the front door, strode to the plastic flaps and through to the connecting door of the greenhouse. Through the steamy window set into the door he could see a tall silhouette moving around in there. The radio was on the shelf outside, and Peter snapped it off.

The door opened to reveal a six foot black caterpillar, rather, Norris trussed up in the black sleeping bag, a long thin roll-up between his lips. It was rather cold, though warm saccharine steam began to hiss out from within the greenhouse.

"Norris, what are you…?"

Norris hopped out in his sleeping bag and flung out an arm behind him to slam the door, but not before Peter saw the sea of cannabis plants half unpacked from an open crate, illuminated under the bright lights.

The caterpillar glowered at Peter. "What are you doing here, Lemon?"

"I came to bring this…" Peter said, lifting the spade a little, "What the heck are you doing in there?"

Norris shuffled towards him so that they were almost nose-to-nose and Peter saw the tip of a trowel spring up from inside the sleeping bag and felt it press against his throat.

"You mind your business." Norris said, "The way I see it, this shop is an O'Sullivan enterprise. No Lemons allowed."

Peter raised the spade.

"You gonna use that?" Norris said.

Peter glared hard at the man, and then felt himself soften. This wasn't him, this wasn't him at all. What was he to do? Would Ade even believe him afterwards?

Norris head-butted him, and he fell to the floor, the spade clattering down next to him.

"I don't want you around no more. Aidan don't want you around neither. So you get out of here, you hear? And don't say nothing."

Peter laid there, momentarily stricken, feeling tears welling up in his eyes.

Norris chuckled, shuffled towards the open back door, and lit the huge joint.

"Cold tonight." He said, blowing a long plume of smoke out over the hole outside, shivering in his dirty, black, sleeping bag.

Animation returned to Peter's body and he clambered to his feet, the spade scraping a little on the concrete floor as he picked it up.

#

The next day Ade arrived to work to find all the lights on and he could hear the radio blaring inside, so loud he could hear it over the noise of the builders, who at least were meant to be finishing up that morning.

He opened the front door and let himself in. The shelves were empty and the till was yet to be filled up with money.

I should've known it wouldn't last. He thought.

"Norris?" He shouted.

Probably can't hear me over this racket, he thought.

"Norris!" He yelled again, heading on through to the back, "This really won't do! All the lights and the noise! We've to pay for electricity you know?"

He grunted as he cast his eyes over the stockroom. It looked as though someone had given it a bit of a clean. The area around the back door, where the builders traipsed in and out, in their muddy boots to use the toilet, had been particularly well scrubbed by the looks of it. He noted that the radio was not on its shelf. Norris had taken it into the greenhouse with him.

"Norris, I appreciate the cleaning but really the noise…"

Ade opened the greenhouse door, and was stuck full force by the uninhibited beat and the sight of a thriving cannabis farm.

#

When Peter arrived at work at the usual time, he found PC Summers at the end of a line of Police Officers leaving the shop.

"Norris." He muttered, rubbing an old wound on his thigh, "I'm going to get that worm."

As the officers piled into their panda cars and whizzed off with their sirens blazing, Peter stepped inside the shop, and found Ade slapping the coins into the till with some degree of violence.

"What's going on?"

"Seems my brother hasn't changed one damn bit!"

He slammed the drawer, held both sides of the till, and shook his head.

"Where is he?" Peter said.

"Who knows? Out somewhere. Doubt he'll be back any time soon now the police have been round. You know how news travels in Grenton."

He met Peter's eye. "Look, Peter I'm sorry about yesterday… how I behaved… Norris…"

"Don't worry about it." Peter said, "Don't worry at all.

"Lemon." Said Ade, a weak smile creeping on to his face.

"Ade." Said Peter, smiling back at him.
"Don't mind if I do."

"Well then let me buy you one tonight. Game of chess down the Bay Horse?"

#

Later that night, as Ade puzzled over the board and Peter sipped his drink, Edgar Wobble came over to collect their empties.

"Back to this, eh, Edgar?" Said Peter.

"Yes." Edgar grunted, "Foreman laid me off straight after we filled in that hole this morning."

"How come?"

"Oh, you know, stupid stuff… 'not the right fit'… 'work ethic'… said he wasn't happy about you throwing five of those black rubbish bags in the hole, when I told him it'd be three or four max. Said nowt at the time. Think he wanted an excuse to fire me. Felt threatened. Knows I'm going places."

He threw his greasy locks back and stared through the window with a dreamy expression on his face.

Across the room sat Gerald, reading from the Grenton Gazette, a pint of mild on the table in front of him, and Bert sniffing around for fallen peanuts by his feet.

His eyes appeared over the top of the newspaper and Peter thought he gave him a slight nod, before disappearing below the top of the paper again.

Peter realised Edgar had wandered off and Ade's eyes were fixed on him.

"What's up?" Said Peter.

"Check."

THE END

Other titles by **BLKDOG Publishing** which you may enjoy.

Citizen Survivor Tales
By Richard Denham

Citizen Survivor's Handbook
By Richard Denham & Steve Hart

The Paranormal Investigations of Mister Balls
By Richard Denham

I'm Not Being Racist, But…
By K. Lee

Blue Crayon
By Rowen Ingrid Parker

Dad Jokes
By K. Lee

Poems of a Broken Soul
By Iza Tirado

Fade

By Bethan White

Sacrosanct: Poems by Prison Survivors

By various authors

Lemonade

By Tom Ashton

Hour of the Jackals

By Emil Eugensen

Soft Hunger

By Lucrezia Brambillaschi

Robin Hood: The Legacy of a Folk Hero

By Robert White

Diary of a Vigilante

By Shaun Curtis

Arthur: Shadow of a God

By Richard Denham

Dark and Light Tales of Ripton Town

By John Decarteret

Mixed Rhythms and Shady Rhymes

By Teresa Fowler

Thin Blue Rhymes

By various authors

Click Bait

By Gillian Philip

The Woe of Roanoke

By Mathew Horton

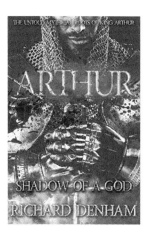

Arthur: Shadow of a God
By Richard Denham

King Arthur has fascinated the Western world for over a thousand years and yet we still know nothing more about him now than we did then. Layer upon layer of heroics and exploits has been piled upon him to the point where history, legend and myth have become hopelessly entangled.

In recent years, there has been a sort of scholarly consensus that 'the once and future king' was clearly some sort of Romano-British warlord, heroically stemming the tide of wave after wave of Saxon invaders after the end of Roman rule. But surprisingly, and no matter how much we enjoy this narrative, there is actually next-to-nothing solid to support this theory except the wishful thinking of understandably bitter contemporaries. The sources and scholarship used to support the 'real Arthur' are as much tentative guesswork and pushing 'evidence' to the extreme to fit in with this version as anything involving magic swords, wizards and dragons. Even Archaeology remains silent. Arthur is, and always has been, the square peg that refuses to fit neatly into the historians round hole.

Arthur: Shadow of a God gives a fascinating overview of Britain's lost hero and casts a light over an often-overlooked and somewhat inconvenient truth; Arthur was almost certainly not a man at all, but a god. He is linked inextricably to the world of Celtic folklore and Druidic traditions. Whereas tyrants like Nero and Caligula were men who fancied themselves gods; is it not possible that Arthur was a god we have turned into a man? Perhaps then there is a truth here. Arthur, 'The King under the Mountain'; sleeping until his return will never return, after all, because he doesn't need to. Arthur the god never left in the first place and remains as popular today as he ever was. His legend echoes in stories, films and games that are every bit as imaginative and fanciful as that which the minds of talented bards such as Taliesin and Aneirin came up with when the mists of the 'dark ages' still swirled over Britain – and perhaps that is a good thing after all, most at home in the imaginations of children and adults alike – being the Arthur his believers want him to be.

Fade
By Bethan White

Do you want to remember?

Do you want to forget?

There is nothing extraordinary about Chris Rowan. Each day he wakes to the same faces, has the same breakfast, the same commute, the same sort of homes he tries to rent out to unsuspecting tenants.

There is nothing extraordinary about Chris Rowan. That is apart from the black dog that haunts his nightmares and an unexpected encounter with a long forgotten demon from his past. A nudge that will send Chris on his own downward spiral, from which there may be no escape.

There is nothing extraordinary about Chris Rowan...

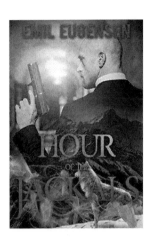

Hour of the Jackals

By Emil Eugensen

It is a time of chaos, a time of vengeance, an hour of jackals.

A shadow stirs. Why is the US president slowly losing his mind? Why is Europe falling apart and why are fascist coups seemingly imminent across the world?

A Chinese spy and his American colleague try to deduce who is behind everything. An English professor makes a Faustian deal to get revenge on his daughter's racist attackers. A young federal agent falls in love with the woman he is ordered to betray. All the while the fascist conspirators are preparing their secret mind-control weapons.

Yet other, possibly supernatural, forces could be at play as well. Including one unearthly Domina, who will provide any information you may seek, but the payment is harsh indeed...

Click Bait

By Gillian Philip

A funny joke's a funny joke. Eddie Doolan doesn't think twice about adapting it to fit a tragic local news story and posting it on social media.

It's less of a joke when his drunken post goes viral. It stops being funny altogether when Eddie ends up jobless, friendless and ostracised by the whole town of Langburn. This isn't how he wanted to achieve fame.

Eddie knows he's blown his relationship with rich girl Lily Cumnock. It's Lily's possessive and controlling father Brodie who fires him from his job - and makes sure he won't find another decent one in Langburn. And Eddie doesn't even have Flo to fall back on - his old nan died some six months ago, and Eddie is still recovering from the death of the woman who raised him and who loved him unconditionally.

Under siege from the press, and facing charges not just for the joke but for a history of abusive behaviour on the internet, Eddie grows increasingly paranoid and desperate. The only people still speaking to him are Crow, a neglected kid who relies on Eddie for food and company, and Sid, the local gamekeeper's granddaughter. It's Sid who offers Eddie a refuge and an understanding ear.

But she also offers him an illegal shotgun - and as Eddie's life spirals downwards, and his efforts at redemption are thwarted at every turn, the gun starts to look like the answer to all his problems.

www.blkdogpublishing.com

Printed in Great Britain
by Amazon